To Cameron, Carmin, and Sage—
my three favorite monsters.
—KK

To my favorite brother.
—GB

Henry Holt and Company, *Publishers since 1866*
Henry Holt® is a registered trademark of Macmillan Publishing Group, LLC.
120 Broadway, New York, New York 10271 • mackids.com

Library of Congress Cataloging-in-Publication Data is available
ISBN 978-1-250-81759-4

Our books may be purchased in bulk for promotional, educational, or business use.
Please contact your local bookseller or the Macmillan Corporate and Premium
Sales Department at (800) 221-7945 ext. 5442 or by e-mail
at MacmillanSpecialMarkets@macmillan.com.

First Edition, 2022
Printed in China by RR Donnelley Asia Printing Solutions Ltd.,
Dongguan City, Guangdong Province
1 3 5 7 9 10 8 6 4 2

A MONSTER IS EATING THIS BOOK!

Words
KAREN KILPATRICK

Pictures
GERMÁN BLANCO

HENRY HOLT
New York

This is a book.

But it's no ordinary book.

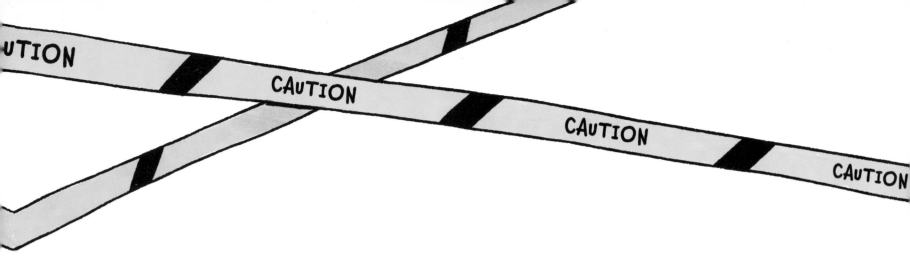

You see, inside this book lives a **MONSTER**... so we have to be **VERY CAREFUL.**

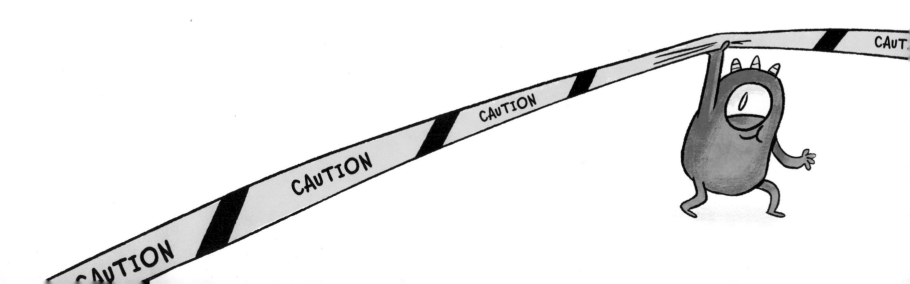

We should probably

whisper.

And try not to laugh too loud at any funny pictures.

We don't want to wake it up.

DANGER
CREATURE
HAZARD

BEWARE

DO NOT
ENTER

WARNING

WARNING

NO
ENTRY

Before we continue, we should probably learn some MONSTER facts.

The MONSTER doesn't eat ordinary **TREATS.**

It makes a **MESS** wherever it goes.

And if you hear a **GROWL** . . .

you have to be ready

to get away **FAST.**

AMAZING!

Now you are an expert on the MONSTer.

OOPS! That was quite loud, wasn't it?

A missing word!

TREATS

MESS

FAST

UH-OH.

We might have a problem now.
The MONSTER that lives inside this book
sleeps a lot, but when it's awake . . .

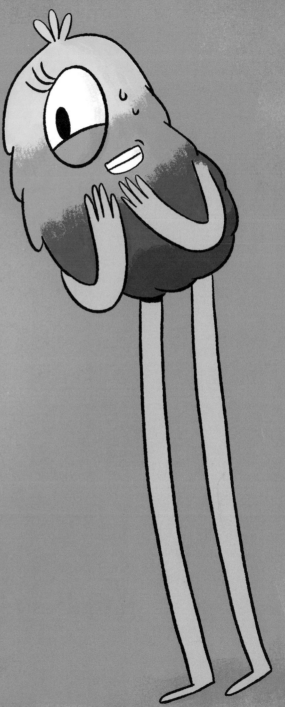

it gets **VERY HUNGRY.**

And just as we like to **READ** words,

it likes to **EAT** words.

Oh no! Another missing word!

TREATS

MESS

But if it's eating the **WORDS,**
how will we ever finish reading the **BOOK?**

WHAT CAN WE DO?

Maybe, just maybe, we can feed it
so many words that it will stuff itself and
be too full to eat anything else.

LET'S TRY!

Here are some words for it to eat.

HAPPY

GROWL

MESS

HUNGRY

HI

BARK

CAN

TWO

FAST

WHAT

TREATS

WALK

WE

TREES

FETCH

HOW

BE

FRIENDS

BUS

Wow, it must be really hungry!

GROWL

HAPPY

HI   BARK

HUNGRY

CAN   TWO

WHAT

WALK   WE   TREES

FETCH

BE

BUS   FRIENDS

OH NO, it's still not full yet?

What will happen if it eats ALL the words . . . ?!?

HI

HUNGRY

CAN

WALK   WE   TREES

BE

FRIENDS

That was unexpected.

Well, we did say this was no

ordinary book

So let's finish reading (and eating) together!

Meet our new

HUNGRY

best **FRIEND.**

THE EN